Eraser

Angharad Williams
ERASER

Edited by Kathrin Bentele

Kunstverein für die Rheinlande und
Westfalen, Düsseldorf

After 8 Books

PROLOGUE

Steady now, full moon.

THE ROOM

At first it was darkness. Bible-black one could say. In truth, it was only oblivion: we'd had it before. I heard lightening's bolt cleave at timber with a deafening taran. Some revival! The strike of it washes me up on grit shores. Some awakening! Thunder continues the tirade – bark cracks, parts, and falls with a thud. It sustains a charge in the air.

At times' insistence my eyes' lubrication had suffocated, with all my moisture turning to a crisp rind on my peepers! I am eager to see! In response to this, each dark-filled sphere secretes a single tear. The volatile liquid trails across the eyes, loosening the soldered lids. I take my time – one peeper follows the other through crispy blinks as the crust dissolves.

As though a thousand pianos were struck all at once I see – now, through narrowed aperture – a dark room illuminated by strobing shadows – lightening revealing its abandoned dimensions. Light lays trapped in liquid droplets suspended on woven gossamer at the room's corners and edges, like a galaxy. My eyes roam and attempt to count the corners of the room. I can't quite reach one; I try moving my neck — no use. I try moving my head

— *oh, no use.*

I am laid on a bed. I am bound to a body.

Ears and eyes activated, I become aware of other body parts — heeding breath's remarkable mechanism: more goes in if I flare the nostrils and the chest goes up, and then down, up, and then down, and needs no reminding! Whilst revelling in the metronomic device and impressed by the whistle from my nose, my eyes soon alert me to an odour from which there is no reprieve.

I am the odour! I sting my *own* eyes! My substance has me entombed! I lay petrified — but! There is a peace to this larval state! From the distinct vacancy of my mind a question emerges — how did I get here?

And, who am — *I*?

Hereby an incredible awareness

courses through to the rest of this body's story here, and I begin to nudge at my extremes: the limbs. The first to rouse are fingers – of course – eager with a wee twitch. The right index digit explores the limits of its cage, flicking at the roof of its detaining caul. Right index gains strength and births, piercing through the membrane with a wet crack. The other fingers follow swiftly and then a forearm as bold as roses is now free. With my chin at my chest I gaze at the tips of long, dark, curled nails. What pleasure it is to stretch them out – an impressive pianist here. Once beaten from their extraction they fall with a bounce on to the bed.

Emboldened in its new role, the hand paws ever so gently at the quilt beneath, fingering at sewn edges and pulling gently at loose cotton thread. On its journey, hand wanders as an aged creepy crawly and stumbles onto something cold and hard! I send out a finger to investigate, I *tap-tap-tap* as cool, hard length becomes two circular squiggles.

A manifest companion next to me!

Cautiously now! There are scissors! What a spooky tool!

Season by season I preserved my position on the horizon of chaos. Against siege of rain and the winds of attrition, I – the prototype – must now release myself from this nick! Evoking dormant force, I take a hold of the scissors, tearing the rest of my arm through the membrane to be freed!

My head's lack of mobility is bothersome. The hair on my head has become attached to a jaundiced pillow – the scissors! The key to my release!

I amble the tip towards my head as it reaches my temple.

Slowly now, wobbler!

They feel so treacherous in my hand, the scissors, and these long finger-claws help little! I struggle and graft awkwardly to prize open the blades, the pivot point rusted and stubborn. I take a deep breath, the moment stabilises, the steel snouts find their starting point. *Chomp* it goes. *Chomp, chomp, chomp* – and in no time at all my head is released from the sticky thatch.

Casting my tool aside I push gently through the yoke to release the upper body. Sit up in bed and, head free, I note that thing rotates at three hundred and sixty degrees! *Weeee!* I count every corner of the room, twice! Untethered, I arrange two makeshift fists with which to break my legs free before rolling onto my side.

Uff, most biblical hangover.

Dwell not. Feet next!

They hover claws first and land on the ground. Despite earnest, slow balancing on the way up, my knees buckle, and I fall to the floor.

'Tis your birthright to stand!

Several professional stumbles later — I am up!

Here I am baby!

I have risen undamaged into this raw day. My cold eyes take measure of the wooden furniture around me, bowed and buckling. Stepping tentatively on soaked carpets, I duck my head beneath wilted garlands of anthracite amulets descending from the ceiling. Knickknacks and trinkets top a dresser which holds gowns of mold in pinks, greens, and browns. Whose life was this? I move for a closer look at the dresser and catch my reflection in the window's glass pane –

Oh! I see! I'm a woman!

I'm a woman.

I'm a woman.

I'm a woman.

I am a woman.

I'm a woman.

I'm a woman.

My skin appears shellacked. With a curious sediment: crystalline and dewy looking. I impulsively reach to touch my face but –

You're really getting in the way!

One last studious look at my curved and twisted, bark-like nails before I snap them off one by one and drop them onto the floor with a clang. With what's left of my blackened digits I tear my mouth open. My tongue is radical now, I taste myself on the muscular rover and take it all in. The woman.

Oh! What is this?

Without warning, I am rendered blind as thin bars move across my field of vision. There are enoki mushrooms jauntily growing out from my nostrils and hooking towards my face! I thought the image would unify me, instead I am multiplied.

What on earth...?

I pick them. One by one but they sprout with speed. I've become a breeding ground for edibles! Is this what's become of me? I cannot wait to see what other fruits will emerge from my body. But I won't be converted to fungus and mould just yet; I see nature's simple equations and they frighten me.

I start to leave the chamber. On my way out I take pause for one last look at my kip patch and see my outline as a Sentinel's position. Now a mere cold shell.

No, I can't take you with – me –

I've shared my health with you long enough, so long in fact that my face is all splintered! Blasts of light echo through the room followed by a billowing roar – what timing!

15

There – you see – I have been served my summons.

Directly outside the chamber, a set of steep stairs leads down to a small kitchen. Bracing myself on a sodden banister as my naked feet play the timbre of tired stairs, I make my way down, knees still weak beneath me.

The room opens up, revealing an impressive fireplace wholly intact; to the right, an aluminium bucket collects rainwater from a wet nipple that protrudes from the ceiling. I jump the final step and march over as thirst thrusts my cupped hands into the bucket and proceed to swallow the liquid with abandon.

I eye the half-open barn door back towards the foot of the stairs. I'm beckoned over and so unwrap myself from around the bucket.

Come closer now – steady.

It appears that the tumult of the tempest has abated. I stand in the quiet, toes tickling the barn door. I peer out from where I stand, at a gate of learning, drenched from the sloppy gulps I just took. The grass glistens as bitumen and the night sky pours into the valley like velvet. A mere hundred yards away a pack of wild dogs with throbbing red ears howl, bothersome, at the moon. They seem so mournful, as though the whole valley were barren. On high: the sky is dense with stars renewing their theme of time and death.

I turn and return to my bucket. In this frenzy I neglect my breathing mechanism and before long, the earth refuses to hold my heart and the sinews stiffen. I fall to the ground just before lights out.

Come to now, come to.

A creature calls and I wake with a yawn that stings the edges of my mouth, so unaccustomed am I to having it open!

Ouch!

I see my toppled bucket and watch as water from the nipple splashes unevenly onto the deck. There is a presence in absence at this shelter. There is no lovely picture nor impressive urn on top of the fireplace, but there is a thick ash sediment on each surface; there is no red glass nor brass, no blue and white china and no porcelain pups. I must leave this place and keep my feet free of the world's net, before I become another home for the dust.

Dawn inches up, the principality of sky lightens. I tug the latch of the door open and stand outside in the yard. Mud as soft as excrement pipes through my toes. It tickles! The dogs have gone. In the distance I can make out the faint sound of water, but not from drains or pipes. It's elemental. Off I go past the surrounding parliament of splintered trees that last night bore passive witness to my entombment.

THE TROUT

On this most sensual land I bounced down a green tide, throat full of pollen, my legs barely catching up with my chest. I follow the trickling sound as it grows louder.

Tones familiar to the unborn (if only they could speak of their last moments of peace) emerge from the truest force of nature: a stream comes into focus, where tossed diamonds leap and learn to dance on the chop. I scurry at its rugged edge, searching for caterpillars on the undersides of weeping willow leaves. Worms, bugs and creepy crawlies go about their business as I play a game of thinking myself into the minds and skins of other things. Heat from a vengeful sun pounds down – I can't think myself her. I tried.

There is a sudden disturbance to this peace as trickle turns to splash. I gasp.

Can I think myself into a splash? It comes and goes so quickly. Something moves beneath the surface of the water – that is otherwise teasing at tranquility. I stand perfectly quiet and still – there is it!

A trout!

Through the water's marbled surface and tendrils of algae I see the trout itself: a head, a flash of silver, and then nothing but ripples in the water and a return to serenity. I throw my body down and wriggle on my belly to the bank, wrapping my fingers around the moist edges of the stream for a stable view. Rather coyly the trout gracefully show themselves to me, as they weave between ribbons of reed grass – I counted!

One, two, three, four, five, six, seven *trout.*

I don't hesitate for long and glide my hand into the water 'til it reaches my funny bone. My trout friends disperse and in recollection of a baby's struggle my feet and legs heave me forwards, hacking at the wet grass beneath my body.

A little closer now.

My waist teeters on the edge as my breast hovers above the surface of the water and it takes all my strength to keep my upper body craned as I sink my arm deeper in the water halfway up to my shoulder. I can see my intervention in the force as the currents kink and circle around my arm! Half a minute went by like half an hour.

I caress the water with my fingers. A little one draws near. I hold my breath. I make her a cradle and she parks herself in my little hand basket. We touch. *Ooh* her pelvic fin tickles my palm. *I want to make you feel good too!*

And I work slowly, massaging the trout. Closing my fingers ever-so-gently around the body, I held the trout, and in this holding, I felt a unification. I could not tell where I ended and the fish began. I recall from a song: 'for every atom belonging to me as good belongs to you'.

One last gentle squeeze from my buttocks and I am moved further forward to gaze into her eyes, careful to continue my rhythmic undulation on her lateral lines. I see her in her trance. I sigh as we tickle each other.

Look at us both!

Here like this: orchestrations of carbon.

23

But there is a betrayal in this moment and the dear trout is wrenched from its habitat. I sink my teeth deep into its flesh and immediately taste and relish the trials of its wild existence. My mouth: oh, symphony of flavour, if only I could sing how she tastes. Bones lodge themselves between my teeth as my jaw clamps harder to take another flesh chunk. Trout tail and head slap my cheeks pink and with two hands I yank her away. I am out of breath from all the excitement, noshing on flesh, trout odour so pungent. I chew and marvel at my noisiness!

Gaining a temporal lucidity, I realise dear trout remains in my hands, and I begin to comprehend the fleshy hole I have made before my eyes!

Oh Trout! Paragon of animals. What have I done? You don't bleed?

She flaps so violently I drop her on the ground. Her gasps slow down. Should I return her? Should I eat her head? Finish her? I could not *look* at dear trout. I ran. I ran in all directions. I tried to take every form and shape so as not to be the murderer. Tried to be a caterpillar, tried to be a bucket, a cat, a horse, a table, a stone. I even tried to be a rose! I wanted to turn back, to undo what I had done, to live life over before the crime. It looks easy to go backwards but it meant taking more chunks from dear trout. It was impossible! I had broken another thread that holds me to the world. I collapsed in mournful ecstasy.

WALTZ

I wake from life's best sleep, jubilant and high off omegas. I rise and pompously pat down the scene of the crime to stop it clinging to my hessian garments. I look away. With every choice lies the possibility of regret. I shan't study the splatter and shall not look back! Goodbye dear trout.

In the beyond, the hills turn bald, and a small town comes into focus. I have quite a way to go before reaching the civilisation ahead and wonder what will greet me there. My stride turns to a skip, I can hardly find a way to manage my excitement. Could I be intoxicated still?

I pause and take in a tall, pointy spire against an expansive backdrop of slag. The slag is sculpted into pyramids built in rows which disappear into and form the horizon line. The mere sight of these structures sends me tumbling headfirst into a small valley. The basin is home to a clearing with a small pond which suspends enormous leathery lily pads. On top of one of the floaters, a dragonfly rests contently. Of what do you dream, dragonfly? Its brilliant chitinous body, intricately decorated in metallic and iridescent tones, bastes in the sun. The sun's light refracts off the bejewelled exoskeleton projecting tiny shards of light onto the lily pad's surface. Mother nature dances with herself and marvels at her ingenuity.

Dragonfly wakes all in a flurry of veined transparent wings. She lifts herself, shivering in midair. Her movements almost impossible to chart, the course she takes is of her own erratic splendour. She flounces with such gumption, unfazed as the sky turns sepia, she pauses inflight before another thrust of movement.

I follow her.

This servant of the snake draws me a short distance from the pond through a green tunnel to a leafy clearing within a grove. Autumn leaves lay all languid here, animated occasionally by little birds bouncing on nature's trampoline. My feet are invisible to me now as I push my shins through the brown and red crush.

Above, mute beams of light make their way through a thick ambush of leaves, illuminating the clearing. The arena is revealed, and its lining is made up of dense rose bushes. At first the bushes appear lifeless, it is only as my shoulder passes that the once gaunt petals become flush with yellow and white, or flourish with peach and purples, crimson at countless edges. The rose buds open and broaden, showing themselves to me.

I speed up, and as I pass further, more and more roses come to life – this cannot be! I lean in for a closer look and to my surprise I see two flowers communicating – one pink rose and one yellow rose, they're playing peek-a-boo! My body jerks back in surprise! Had I imagined these two gregarious playmates? With hands on knees I hinge at my hips waiting with bated breath until pink turns to me! She holds her two petals over herself then
BOO!

I instinctively place my hands over my eyes, parting my fingers and then

Peek-a-boo!

I fall back on the leafy mattress, my sides splitting with laugher. All the while the flower tries to hoist herself up! I rise to witness her press her thick bottom leaves against the surrounding bramble. Her leaves shake from the heaving,

Oh, you wanna come up?

She pushes with such effort, I wrap my right hand around his thorny stalk and yank him away from his friends. I hold the rose to my nose to take in her scent as she tenderly holds my cheeks with her petals circling the outline of my face as her stalk grows bigger and bigger until I can no longer hold her in one hand! I take hold with both hands, and one of his outer petals falls onto my face, covering it entirely. I inhale deeply and almost suffocate as the petal plunges into my nose and mouth. Her stalk is now so big that she is my size, standing in front of me, and gaining still!

I hear the timpani, I feel it too.

All of my outsides goose-skinned, and the little hairs stood to attention, I breathe so loud and deep; I feel an ache. *What is the meaning of this?* Rose and I caress our visages onto one another.

Because she is now so big, I take hold of two opposing thorns at her neck and climb her like a ladder, my legs dangling — I mount my soft, chubby calves, impaling them onto Rose. Squeezing tight, he takes flight, and we are airborne!

We twist and launch through our wooded shelter up into the sky. Hot, red liquid oozes from where I am punctured and runs down my ankles. Such bliss made my chest hot to the touch and flooded my mind with memories; images of such banality flashed before me as though tuning a radio. Lasting from the static: an overwhelming recollection of noxious grief and a funereal walk up the stairs to the room. I see through these eyes to my mind's eye: a past life. Some body's life. It must be mine. Memories become fused with blood as my heart pounds. I see to the point of blindness and then an incredible release! My spheres so full of the dark again and yet my head so light it could fall off!

The sepia sky turns to crystal. I rest my cheek on Rose's stalk, exhausted from our exchange. I don't *think* anything, instead, I recall and replay in my mind our encounter – and ponder over which action led to the other and so on. I reminisce about the delicacy of her petal on my lips and how I could hardly breathe from his aroma. We catch our breath above the clouds before winding down and back to earth again. The trampoline braces our fall and we lay there in silence.

My legs pop off where I was attached to Rose and I sit up to examine the wounds. During this prudent moment I mull over the memories brought to me by our ecstasy: how can I begin to understand them? I tear away a giant blade of grass to wrap tight around the gashes. She must sense my brooding. She makes an overture to me, resting a leaf tenderly before tugging at my arm, gently drawing me back. Seeking answers in my face I explain — I have many questions! Rose quips that questions are a burden to others: answers are a prison for oneself. He swaddles my body in her thick leaves and we nap. The best thing in life is to be remembered. I don't wake her to say goodbye.

THE MINER

With what voracity did I plunge onto the cobbled streets!

I could hardly believe the stone, how hard and unforgiving it was beneath my bare feet. A cobbled path led up a gentle hill lined with tight rows of narrow houses. I pass a decrepit shop stripped of assets, barely a handful of tins scattered throughout, with no patronage in sight. Some foreclosed future!

Alone here — I take pause! Turning around to catch a glimpse of the trip so far: it was too beautiful to capture at the moment of seeing. Ageless, the colours renewed with each passing moment variations of light and distance that no artist could paint nor suggest. A view for the few, apparently.

Barrel chested I boing back into this strangely familiar civilisation — a place that has become fragile and ashen. Leafless trees grow from impossible angles, reaching out from cobble, brick and mortar. Splintered and twisted they don't reach for the sun, but are rather drawn in multiple directions, contorted as though gravity had malfunctioned. I weave my way between them.

While walking in this inert town, a bell tolls, and suddenly, this quiet valley becomes ambushed by a crowd of miners. Kings of the underworld! The miners' bodies pollute the street and I'm gently pushed past as hostile eyes penetrate my gaze. They look down on me from below! I look over their muscular buttocks and bowlegs with admiration.

As they weave through the network of trees, I mimic their arrogant strut. I want to be like them, aristocrats of the working class. Disheveled and rowdy, their clothes waxy and thick. I wonder, in the dead of night, do these garments animate and walk themselves proud about town? It's hard to tell if they're part of my story or if I'm a part of theirs. I follow them, and nose first, thanks to their formidable pong.

In this inert town time crawls on its hands and knees.

The crowd disperses, some into little houses, others through the bat-winged entrance of a pub. Tugged by the nose, I find myself astonished at the scene before me. Suffice to say celebration is in the air. There is tinkering at the piano whose keys, so well worn, are entirely black. Throughout, voracious chat continues with the tendency to cascade into a roar, and the waves repeat as though a child were at the volume's dial.

The pack intimidates me somewhat, but keen to prove I am not some corporate outlier I must try to engender myself to them. I pluck up the courage. Pushing past the swinging doors, I make my way through the partygoers, grinning and nodding in time with the tinkering keys. My nods are respectfully answered with doffing of caps or a wink here and there. I peel my feet off the sticky floor one step at a time before reaching the bar, and the biggest barrel of all. He sits alone, set away from the rowdy singing and play fighting. He seems surprised at my proximity and leans back on his stool, drink still firmly in hand.

Once composed he declares

Quite a shearing that.

Although rather bemused by his words I understand he is talking about my hair as he dabs at his own with stained fingers at his head.

Aye, one way o' gettin ye' self off tha' bed.

He knows me. He rotates on his stool and glares into his brown transparent drink. We share a little silence.

Bin eatin' 'ave yew?

He speaks like a song – pointing to a mirror at the end of the bar, so I go over to seek my reflection – between closed lips, fine bones peek out gleaming like gossamer of dearest you-know-who! Smile! I pull and yank out the cluster.

Ano'er one! And f'our guest!

He declares, before emptying the contents of his glass into his throat. I return to him. Over the surface of his forehead, he asks me where I'd been. He cared little for my response, fanning the words away as though they were little flies circling his face looking for a spot to land! He remains generous nevertheless, smiling in my direction, nudging my drink towards me. Finally, our eyes meet. His globes held tribulation akin to the tree's rings, and when I took him in I learnt about grief.

It is beyond the word.

The globes: perfect black. So much so I cannot tell if I am, in fact, staring into the sockets themselves. The flesh around them moves, mimicking my expression of ocular exploration. And now we are synchronised; assessing one another like dogs.

I frown, he frowns.

Something small but sharp drops onto my foot – a tooth!

They cascade out onto the ground and the rest in my head – I swallowed there and then.

Socketed man watches. His sockets are as black as his voice is loud.

'ats how it starts yew see?
he goes.

'Ew won' be needin' 'em much longer.

The ramblings of the socketed man continue with certain words coming up for air amidst the drink-powered drivel. He speaks of some distorted gravity that took his teeth, and intermittently mentions a great big black hole. He asks about my infancy, but I chase after the hole. His response is to send out a rogue blackened index, and he draws a circle in the air.

We've be'n drilling, see.

In this inert town shadows are suspended on dust. This place was fated to die.

Decided, 'et's push things along abit!

He makes a monocle with thumb and index finger with which to look through and at me. He tears into another roar

Ano'er one!

Slamming shots of brown liquid, I am no longer jubilant, but rather troubled by my encounter. The barkeeper taps me on

the shoulder. They explain with perfect
lucidity—

*They're celebrating reaching the
core this morning. All those precious met-
als will come pouring up soon. It ought to
cover the entire surface of the Earth with
a metre-thick layer of gold and platinum.*

With a broad smile

You can go and see it if you like!

This denuded town is the capitol of
dusk.

THE MAGPIE

With instruction from the barkeeper, I move at haste to find the hole to watch as earth takes her last gasp. There is no present here and no future neither – only the past brittle with relics. The church's bells have ceased to chime.

The hole is encircled by a fence. I hear and feel rumblings from the greatest darkness below. Atop a fencepost stands an adorned magpie. Cocky – its tail wags rude and ginger: donned and adorned with the best jewels: tales of other people's lives. Stolen dress, bloated prizes. It moults no feathers at its shameless looting.

Beneath it on the ground are a trail of talismans and trophies leading to the hole, and with a voice full of money, the magpie makes its call. Why would anyone abide such an archivist? I mull the perfect riposte.

I *had* thought the best thing was to be remembered. But memories are merely another possession.

To satisfy my distain I secure both hands around the bird, squeeze its body hard and shove its head in my mouth, gnawing at the neck. I feel my gums shattering its tiny bones – it's an effort but I succeed after several attempts to release the head from its body.

I chew the beak and all the rest like bubble gum, cock my head back taking in the last of the perfect, elastic blue sky and launch out the transformation. I raise magpie above my head and wring its body like a wet flannel over my face; magpie's blood, organs and sinews fall into my mouth and over my chin, which is covered now and I am crimson bearded.

This was no inert town! Duped was I! It has sought its own death and perhaps this was not entirely sad. Back to oblivion, again.

REMEMBER ME ROSE!

INDEX

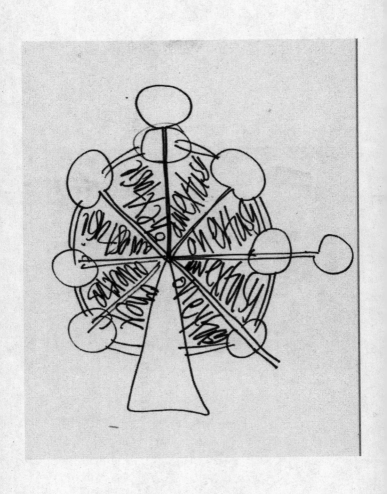

[1]

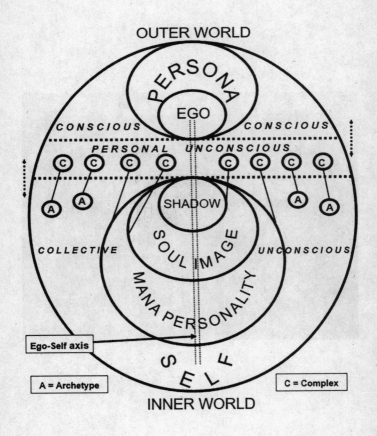

OUTER WORLD

PERSONA

EGO

CONSCIOUS   CONSCIOUS

PERSONAL UNCONSCIOUS

C C C C   C C C C

A A   SHADOW   A A

COLLECTIVE   SOUL IMAGE   UNCONSCIOUS

MANA PERSONALITY

Ego-Self axis

SELF

A = Archetype   C = Complex

INNER WORLD

[3]

[4]

[6].

[8]

[10]

[11]

Spinning Wheels for Yarn, Flax and Silk, shown at the Welsh Fireside Industries
Exhibition at Lampeter.

[14]

[15]

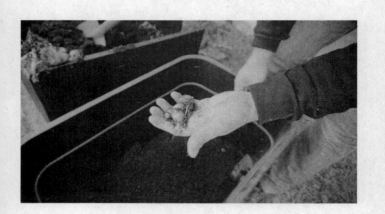

[17]

[18]

[1] Angharad Williams, sketch, 2020, felt tip on paper.

[2] Angharad Williams, *Trout, Paragon*, 2020, oil on canvas.

[3] Carl Gustav Jung, *Model of the Psyche and Psychological Development*, n.d.

[4] Nancy Sinatra and Lee Hazlewood, *Some Velvet Morning*, 1967, video still.

[5] Lawrence Alma-Tadema, *The Roses of Heliogabalus*, 1888, oil on canvas.

[6] Angharad Williams, *Now Watch this drive*, 2017, performance.

[7] Angharad Williams, *We Will Never die*, 2015, image from behind the camera.

[8] Georgios Iakovidis, *Kou-Kou*, 1895, oil on canvas.

[9] Metal porcupine figure owned by Sigmund Freud, manufactured by Franz Bergman Factory, Vienna.

[10] Angharad Williams, *Joe Public*, 2022, video still.

[11] Angharad Williams, *Joe Public*, 2022, video still.

[12] Spinning wheels for yarn, flax, and silk shown at the Welsh Fireside Industries Exhibition organized by the Lampeter Section of the Cardiganshire Antiquarian Society, held at the Town Hall, Lampeter, in December 1913.

[13] Angharad Williams, *Gate to the Vegetable garden, Rhianfa*, 2021.

[14] Richard Burton and his father Dic Jenkins crossing the bridge 'Y Bont Fawr' in Pontrhydyfen, 1953.

[15] Image of Aberfan disaster, 1966, photo: BBC/PA.

[16] Angharad Williams, *Nature is nature is nature but also so much more depending on your perspective*, 2021, video still.

[17] Angharad Williams, *Nature is nature is nature but also so much more depending on your perspective*, 2021, video still.

[18] Angharad Williams, *Cars (detail of 'Fiat Panda')*, 2022, charcoal on paper.

AFTERWORD
Kathrin Bentele

Angharad Williams' *Eraser* exists as a book, an exhibition, and a performance that all coincided with her exhibition at Kunstverein für die Rheinlande und Westfalen, Düsseldorf in 2022. *Eraser* addresses the categorical boundaries of our consensual reality—the lines we usually draw between self and other, human and non-human, waking and dreaming consciousness—, and emphasizes an urge to overcome them. It attends to the relationship between inner and outer worlds and the marks, both destructive and curative, that we irrevocably leave on our surrounding worlds in every step and decision we take—and the marks those worlds leave on us. The main protagonist in *Eraser* undergoes multiple transformations via psychic and physical transferences with elementary forces—involving a trout and a magpie, among other things. A desire to give herself up to these forces at one point turns sensuality into violence, thus revealing dynamics of power and submission at play in the human outlook of the world. If capitalism suggests to consider subject-object relations primarily in terms of ownership and property, *Eraser* invites us to imagine other forms of encounter. Here, the categorical distinctions between individual self, others, and non-human life slowly begin to dissolve.

IMAGE CREDITS

[1, 2, 6, 7, 10, 11, 13, 16, 17] Angharad Williams

[3] https://watchwordtest.com/dynamics, last accessed: January 9, 2023.

[4] https://www.youtube.com/watch?v=670YMraVnyk, last accessed: January 9, 2023.

[5] https://commons.wikimedia.org/wiki/File:The_Roses_of_Heliogabalus.jpg, last accessed: January 9, 2023].

[8] https://commons.wikimedia.org/wiki/File:Kou-Kou_by_Georgios_Iakovidis.jpg, last accessed: January 9, 2023.

[9] © Freud Museum London [https://www.freud.org.uk/collections/objects/3146, last accessed: January 9, 2023].

[12] https://ceredigionhistory.wales/spinning-wheels-for-yarn-flax-and-silk-shown-at-the-welsh-fireside-industries-exhibition-at-lampeter, last accessed: January 9, 2023.

[14] © The South Wales Evening Post [https://richardburtonmuseum.weebly.com/pontrhydyfen-and-port-talbot.html, last accessed: January 9, 2023].

[15] Photo: BBC/PA [https://www.the guardian.com/media/greenslade/2016/oct/20/aberfan-a-reporters-letter-home-reveals-the-true-horror-of-the-tragedy, last accessed: January 9, 2023].

[18] Angharad Williams, photo: Cedric Mussano.

This book is published following Angharad Williams' exhibition *Eraser* at Kunstverein für die Rheinlande und Westfalen, Düsseldorf, September 2 to November 27, 2022, curated by Kathrin Bentele.

Text: Angharad Williams
Editor: Kathrin Bentele
Copy-Editor: Rachael Allen
Design: Dan Solbach
Typeface: Minjong Kim
Printing: ScandBook

Acknowledgements: Aimé Césaire, Dylan Huw, Sophia Leiby, Laurence Piercy, R.S. Thomas, Dylan Thomas.

Published by
Kunstverein für die Rheinlande und
Westfalen, Düsseldorf
www.kunstverein-duesseldorf.de
After 8 Books, Paris
www.after8books.com

Distribution:
France & Belgium: Interart, Paris
www.interart.fr
United Kingdom: Art Data, London
www.artdata.co.uk
Rest of Europe: After 8 Books, Paris
www.after8books.com/publishing
The Americas, Asia, and Australia: DAP|
Distributed Art Publishers, New York
www.artbook.com

Supported by:

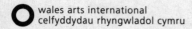

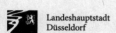

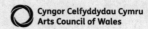

This publication is the fifth in the *singles* series from After 8 Books

ISBN: 9782492650079

Dépôt légal: Septembre 2023